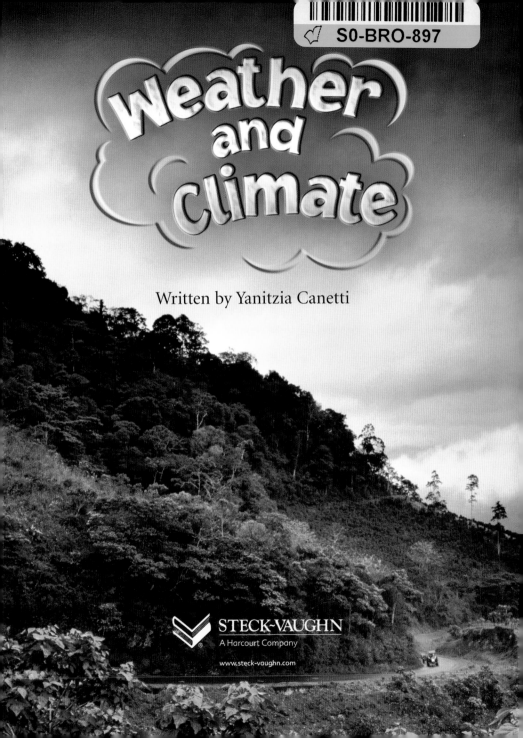

Weather and Climate

Written by Yanitzia Canetti

STECK-VAUGHN
A Harcourt Company

www.steck-vaughn.com

CONTENTS

CHAPTER 1

Weather and Climate: What's the Difference?

What Causes Weather?

Lightning bolts split the sky. Tornadoes lift houses and animals high into the air. Hurricanes bring rain that flood cities near the ocean. The hot sun beats down on desert lands. We know that the earth has many different kinds of weather. We know that weather changes from one day to the next, too. Sometimes it changes during a single day. To know what causes weather, we look at three things—temperature, **air pressure,** and **humidity.**

Temperature is how hot or cold something is. People measure temperature in degrees Fahrenheit (F) and in degrees Celsius (C). The earth's temperature is caused by the sun, and weather really begins with the sun. It gives off energy. The amount of the sun's energy that reaches the earth is different in different places.

Equator

Su

How the sun's rays hit the earth's surface

Countries near the center of the earth get the strongest sunshine, so they are the hottest. Countries farther away from the **equator** are cooler. The uneven heating of the earth causes air to move and makes weather.

Air pressure is the weight of the air that surrounds the earth. Changes in air pressure are mostly caused by changes in temperature. Cold air is dense and causes high pressure. Warm air is less dense and has low pressure. When the pressure is high, the weather is usually mild—not too hot or cold. When the pressure begins to fall, it usually means that a storm is coming. Air moves from areas of high pressure to areas of low pressure. This movement of air is what we call wind.

Humidity is the amount of water in the air. When **water vapor** in the air cools, it **condenses,** or changes to a liquid. The vapor forms tiny droplets. The droplets form clouds. Clouds are a clear signal that the weather is going to change. Clouds usually tell us that we will have **precipitation**—rain, snow, or sleet.

Changes in the weather happen when giant clumps of air move around. These giant clumps of air are called air masses. Each is like the land or water over which it forms. Wet air masses form over water. Air masses that form near the center of the earth are warm.

Air masses don't mix together when they meet. They form what's called a front. When a cold air mass catches up with a warm one, the cold one forces the warm air up into the **atmosphere.** The warm air cools and forms clouds. These clouds often make lightning, thunder, and much rain in a short time.

If a mass of warm air catches up to a cold one, the warm air slides up over the colder air. Clouds form. Then steady rain or snow may fall.

Sometimes fronts stop moving. The rain or snow continues to fall over several days. It can cause flooding and many inches of snow.

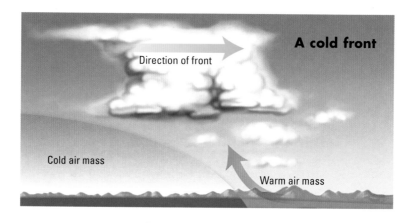

A cold front

Direction of front

Cold air mass

Warm air mass

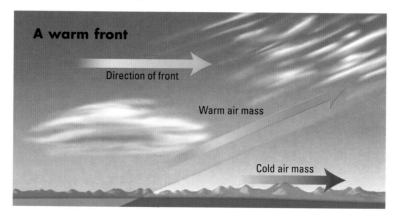

A warm front

Direction of front

Warm air mass

Cold air mass

What Is Climate?

An area's **climate** is the kind of weather it usually has. The main difference between weather and climate is time. An area's weather changes from day to day; an area's climate is its **average** weather over a long period of time.

An area's climate depends partly on its **latitude.** Its latitude is its distance north or south of the equator. The sun shines straight at the equator. The strong sunshine makes the equator very hot. The farther a place is from the equator, the colder it is. The coldest places are the North and South Poles.

The earth has three main climate zones. The temperature of each zone depends on its latitude. The amount of precipitation varies throughout each climate zone. The result is different climates within a zone. For example, the tropical zone has some very wet areas known as tropical rain forests. It also has some very dry areas called tropical deserts.

Namib Desert, a tropical desert in Africa

Climate Zones of the Earth

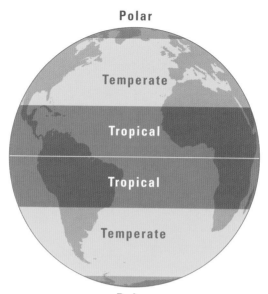

Climate Zone	Temperature	Annual Precipitation
Tropical	Greater than 65° F (18° C) year-round	70–100 in. (180–250 cm) in wet climate; as little as 10 in. (25 cm) in desert climate
Temperate	Up to 110° F (43° C) in summer; below 0° in winter	15–60 in. (38–152 cm)
Polar	Average temperature of warmest month is below 50° F (10° C)	5–15 in. (13–38 cm)

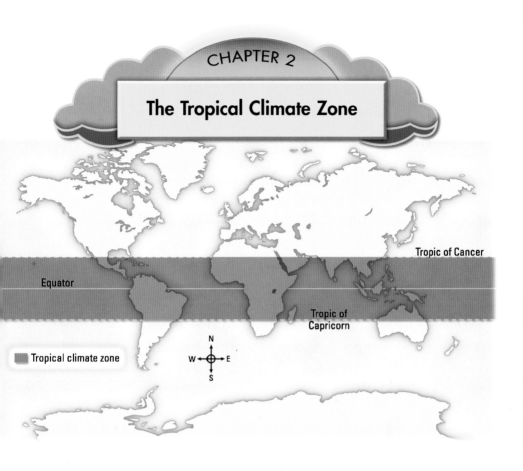

CHAPTER 2

The Tropical Climate Zone

Tropic of Cancer

Equator

Tropic of Capricorn

Tropical climate zone

N
W ← ⊕ → E
S

Can you imagine a place that's hot day and night, all year long? That's what it's like in the tropical zone, or **tropics.** The tropics lie between two lines of latitude on either side of the equator. These lines are called the Tropic of Cancer and the Tropic of Capricorn.

About half of the world's people live in the tropical climate zone. Maybe that's because they would rather live where the weather is sunny and warm.

Not all tropical climates are exactly the same, though. In fact, the tropics have rain forests, grasslands, and deserts!

The Tropical Rain Forest

Tropical rain forests receive more rain than any other climate in the world. These areas are very humid. That means the air is nearly full of water. It is like a sponge that has soaked up all the water it can hold. When a sponge is full, the water drips out. When the air is full of water, the water falls to the earth as rain. The sun and rain in tropical rain forests are wonderful for plants. Four fifths of the world's tropical rain forests are covered with trees and other plants.

A tropical rainforest in Puerto Rico

Rain forests have some of the highest temperatures in the world. They often reach well over 100° F (38° C). Average temperatures are almost 80° F (27° C).

- Up to 32 feet (10 meters) of rain can fall in a tropical rain forest in one year. That's enough to fill a lake!
- Tropical rain forests cover a very small part of the earth, but they are home to more than half of the world's animal and plant species!

Many different animals live in tropical rain forests. Animals as big as a gorilla and as small as an ant make the rain forest their home. Some fly, like the flying dragon lizard and the blue bird of paradise. Others climb trees, like the orangutan. Still others, like the chameleon, crawl. Some are covered with scales, like the tiny vine snake. Some move as quickly as a deer. Others move as slowly as a turtle.

Some of the strangest plants in the world grow in tropical rain forests. One group of odd plants is the carnivorous plants. This group includes the Venus flytrap, a plant that catches and eats flies. In Asia the rafflesia plant lives on the floor of the rain forest, far below the treetops. This plant makes the largest flower in the world. It grows to be the size of a car tire!

The Tropical Grassland

In a rain forest, rain falls all year round. Tropical grasslands have a rainy season and a dry season. Tropical grasslands are not as hot as rain forests. The average temperature is 68° F (20° C). Tall grasses and scattered trees grow on grasslands.

In some tropical areas, strong winds called **monsoons** sweep across the grassland. Monsoons change direction with the season. They can be caused by changes in pressure and by warm and cool air masses coming together. In India and Southeast Asia,

Tropical grassland in South America

Monsoons often cause flooding in India.

the winds change direction twice a year. When the winds come from the land, they are usually dry. When they change direction, though, they blow across the Indian Ocean. There they pick up lots of water. The wind carries the water across the land. There it falls as heavy rain.

The Tropical Desert

Some parts of the tropics are dry. The sun **scorches** the earth. Strong winds carry sand and dirt across the land. Rain almost never falls, and few plants can live. These places are called tropical deserts. Most tropical deserts lie between 15° and 30° latitude. They usually get less than 10 inches (25 centimeters) of rain a year. Temperatures can rise to more than 130° F (55° C). That's hot enough to fry an egg!

- The Sahara Desert in northern Africa is the largest desert in the world. It's as big as the United States!
- Desert sand dunes can stand as high as 330 feet (100 meters)!

The tropical desert may not sound like a nice place to live. Still, plants, animals, and even some people call it home. Half of Australia is covered by desert. Many people have learned to live in Australia's desert.

A tropical desert in Australia

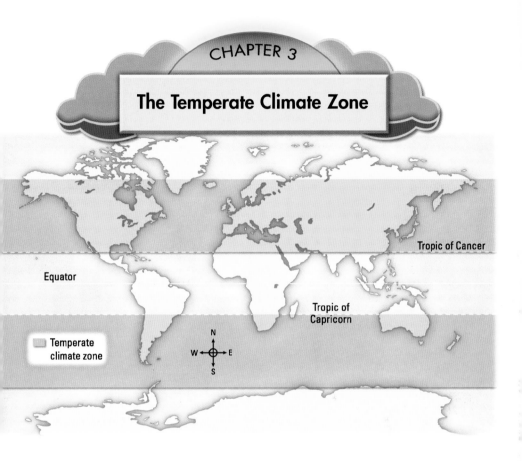

CHAPTER 3

The Temperate Climate Zone

Tropic of Cancer

Equator

Tropic of Capricorn

Temperate climate zone

N
W ← → E
S

The word *temperate* means "not too hot or cold." Places with a temperate climate don't always have nice weather, though. Summer temperatures can reach up to 110° F (43° C). Winter temperatures can drop below freezing.

Places in the temperate climate zone have seasons. The weather changes with the seasons. Why do the seasons change? Let's find out.

The seasons change as the earth moves around the sun.

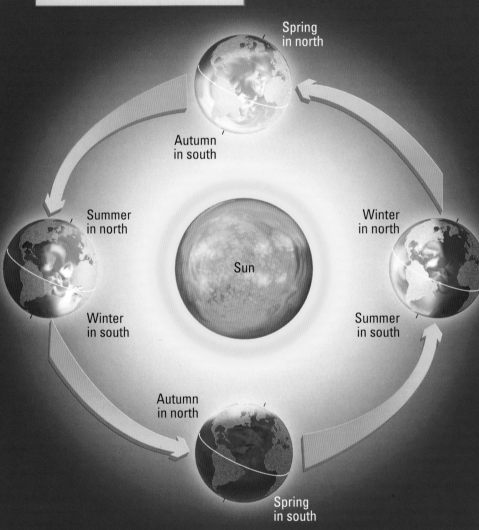

Spring
in north

Autumn
in south

Summer
in north

Winter
in south

Sun

Winter
in north

Summer
in south

Autumn
in north

Spring
in south

The earth moves around the sun. As it moves, the amount of sunlight that reaches different parts of the world changes. The temperature in different parts of the world changes, too. Changes in sunlight and temperature cause changes in seasons. Some places on the earth have four seasons: spring, summer, fall, and winter. Temperate climates have only two clear seasons—warm and cold. The temperatures in these two seasons can be very different.

Dry Temperate Climate

Some places with a temperate climate are dry. These places are usually on the west side of continents. Southern California is on the western coast of the United States. It doesn't get much rain. Like other dry temperate places, it gets between 15 and 40 inches (38–101 centimeters) of rain every year.

Humid Temperate Climate

Places with a humid, or wet, temperate climate are usually on the east side of continents. The southeastern part of the United States has a humid temperate climate.

Winters in Spain are quite cool, but summers are hot.

Areas with a humid temperate climate get rain all year round. They average between 30 and 60 inches (76–152 centimeters) of rain per year. Average summer temperatures are in the low 80s (high 20s C). Winters are short, but temperatures sometimes fall below freezing.

- Some humid temperate climates get at least 10 times as much rain during the wettest summer month as they do in the driest winter month!
- Southern Japan has a humid temperate climate. Summers there are almost as hot as those of the humid tropics. In the winter, cold polar air masses bring frost.

Plants in Temperate Climates

Like people, plants adapt to the weather where they live. Most places with a temperate climate have **deciduous** forests. Southern pines, oaks, magnolias, cypresses, Spanish moss, some palms, and insect-eating plants live in these forests. Evergreen forests are also common in temperate climates. Many evergreen trees grow in the temperate parts of the United States.

The pine tree is a kind of evergreen tree that grows in temperate climates.

CHAPTER 4

The Polar Climate Zone

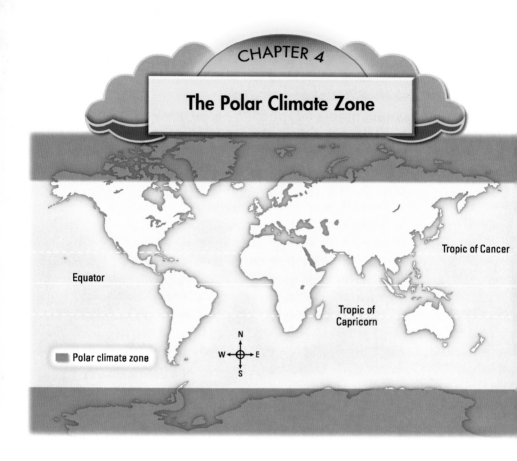

Tropic of Cancer

Equator

Tropic of Capricorn

Polar climate zone

N
W—⊕—E
S

Can people live at a temperature of −70° F (−56° C)? That's how cold it can get in the polar climate zone. The coldest areas are around the North and South poles. Snow and ice cover the land all year at the poles. Summer temperatures rarely rise above freezing!

Not all of the polar climates are so harsh. Some climates around the poles support plants and animals. These areas are called the **taiga** and the **tundra.**

No two snowflakes are the same.

The Taiga

Taiga is a fancy name for a coniferous forest. A coniferous forest is a forest of cone-bearing trees such as spruce, fir, and pine. The taiga receives about 15 inches (38 centimeters) of rain and snow per year.

The Tundra

The polar tundra lies beyond the Arctic Circle on the northern edge of North America and Eurasia. This area gets less than 15 inches (38 centimeters) of rain per year. That's almost like drinking just one glass of water every three months! There are no trees. Much of the soil never thaws out. Still, during the short summer, some plants do manage to grow.

The Polar Ice Caps

The polar ice caps are the coldest places in the world. Their average temperature is below freezing. Almost all of Antarctica and much of the Arctic are polar ice caps.

The Inuit people, or Eskimos, live in a polar area. They have more than 14 different words for snow! Anuik is snow used for drinking water. Maujaq is deep, soft snow. Pukak is dry, granular snow.

Believe it or not, the polar ice caps are very dry. Less than 5 inches (13 centimeters) of snow per year fall on these areas. The ice caps can be as dry as the hot deserts of the tropical climate zone!

Ice and the Earth's Climate

The polar areas form most of the **cryosphere**—the land and sea that are usually covered by snow and ice. The cryosphere helps cool down the earth.

Most land on the earth reflects about one third of the sunlight that hits it. Snow and ice reflect much more light. Some parts of the Antarctic reflect up to

- Antarctica recorded the world's lowest temperature of −128.6° F (−89.2° C) in July 1983.
- In the summer at the North Pole and from November to January at the South Pole, the sun shines until midnight. In the winter, the poles are always dark!

nine tenths of the sun's light. If these polar areas did
not reflect so much sunlight, the earth would absorb
more energy. Its temperature would rise, and the
climate would change.

Scientists use ice to study the history of the earth's
climate. They use long metal pipes to take samples of
ice from the poles. The samples show many layers of
ice. Scientists test the layers to see how old they are.
They check to see how quickly the ice piled up. They
also look for plants and ash from volcanoes in the ice.
These remains tell scientists what the climate was like.
From their tests, scientists know that 100 million years
ago, during the age of the dinosaurs, the earth had very
little snow or ice. The earth's temperature was much
warmer than it is today.

Polar Animals

People do not live in most places with a polar climate. Few plants can live there either. With such cold temperatures, it's not hard to guess

The ermine is a member of the weasel family.

why! Only a few animals can live in the coldest areas. These animals' bodies and ways of living help them to stand the cold.

One interesting animal that lives in polar climates is the musk ox. Musk oxen have lived on earth for more than a million years. They have long, shaggy fur. Under the fur is a coat of wool. The Inuit people use this wool to make cloth. Other land animals, such as polar bears, ermines, and Arctic foxes, also live in polar areas. These three animals all have white fur to match the ice and snow!

Penguins and seals spend time on the ice, too. They have thick, waterproof skin. These animals find their

- Three fourths of the earth's water is stored in **glaciers,** which are found in polar climates.
- Rubies and other gems may lie hidden under Antarctica's thick ice cap!

food in the ocean. Penguins can dive as much as 164 feet (50 meters) below the water to catch fish. That's as deep as a 24-story building is tall! The oceans of polar areas are full of life. Killer whales live in very cold waters.

Penguins live only in Antarctica and surrounding areas. They do not live at the North Pole.

25

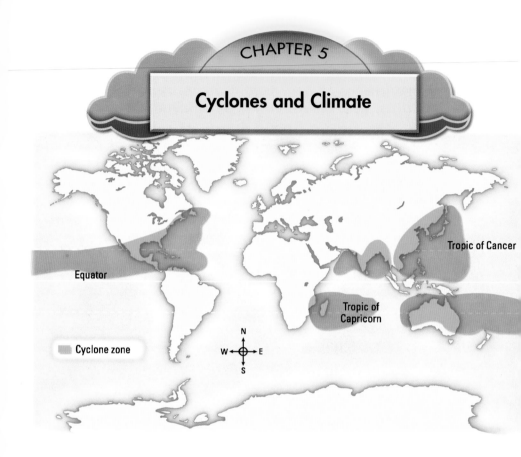

CHAPTER 5

Cyclones and Climate

Tropic of Cancer

Equator

Tropic of Capricorn

Cyclone zone

N
W ⊕ E
S

Cyclones are storms that have different names in different parts of the world. They are called hurricanes in North America. In Asia they are called typhoons. cyclones cause millions of dollars' worth of damage every year. The air in these storms whirls at more than 125 miles (200 kilometers) per hour. An area of very low pressure lies at the center of the whirling wind. This area is called the "eye" of the storm.

Naming Cyclones

When weather forecasters talk about cyclones, they call them by human names. Hugo and Andrew are two famous cyclones. People give names to cyclones to make them easier to track. Giving cyclones names lets people tell the difference between two storms happening at the same time.

Cyclones in Different Climates

Cyclones form at different latitudes and in different climate areas. Different areas have different types of storms. Tropical cyclones are the most powerful storms on the earth. Every year, 80 to 100 cyclones form over tropical oceans. These cyclones have strong winds. They bring very heavy rains. Most of these storms form in late summer and early fall.

Cyclones that form in temperate climates are sometimes called mid-latitude cyclones. These cyclones usually form during the winter. They bring rain or snow to the coasts.

In some polar climate areas, cyclones form year-round. In fact, most of the snow in these regions comes from cyclones.

Damage caused by Hurricane Andrew

The Worst Cyclones

Most tropical cyclones last about seven days. Sometimes, though, they last as long as three weeks. Many cyclones form in the Southern Hemisphere. About ten form in Australia every year. Bangladesh often has terrible cyclones. In 1970 a cyclone with winds up to 143 miles (230 kilometers) per hour struck a town on the coast of Bangladesh. It caused a great deal of damage. In Australia, Cyclone Tracy struck on Christmas Eve, 1974. The region received 7 inches (18 centimeters) of rain in $8\frac{1}{2}$ hours. The winds blew at speeds up to 155 miles (249 kilometers) per hour. The cyclone destroyed much of the area.

World's Deadliest Tropical Storms

Year	Place	Lives Lost
1970	East Pakistan	200,000
1991	Bangladesh	131,000
1965	East Pakistan	47,000
1942	India	40,000
1963	East Pakistan	22,000
1780	West Indies	20,000–22,000
1977	India	20,000
1906	Japan	10,000

Worst United States Hurricanes

Name	Year	Place	Results
None	1900	Texas	6000–8000 lives lost
None	1928	Florida	1836 lives lost
Audrey	1957	Louisiana and Texas	390 lives lost
Camille	1969	Mississippi to Virginia	256 lives lost; almost $13 billion in damage
None	1926	Florida and Alabama	243 lives lost; almost $84 billion in damage
Diane	1955	North Carolina to New England	184 lives lost
Agnes	1972	Florida to New York	117 lives lost; $12 billion in damage
Hugo	1989	North and South Carolina	86 lives lost; almost $13 billion in damage

Cyclones in the United States

The United States has its own cyclones. Some of them form in the northeastern part of the country. What are they called? Northeasters, of course! Northeasters are mid-latitude cyclones. The winds in a northeaster come from the northeastern United States. The storm spins in a counterclockwise motion. It brings water from the Atlantic Ocean and drops it over the land as rain and snow.

This blizzard struck a town in Massachusetts.

In the United States, strong snowstorms are called **blizzards.** In order for a storm to be a blizzard, it must have strong winds and lots of snow. The winds must reach 35 miles (56 kilometers) per hour. The snowfall rate must reach 2 inches (5 centimeters) per hour. Temperatures must fall to near 0° F (−17° C), and visibility must be less than $\frac{1}{4}$ mile (402 meters). Many of the worst blizzards in the United States start in the Gulf of Mexico. The air over the Gulf is warm and moist. The warm, moist air mixes with cold air from the north. This mixture creates the energy needed to form monster storms.

Blizzards pile up huge snowdrifts. In the blizzard of 1888, some snowdrifts were as tall as 20 feet (6 meters)! These storms may seem exciting. Schools close down and people have to stay home. Blizzards can cause a lot of trouble, though. They tear down power lines, damage buildings, and strand people far from home.

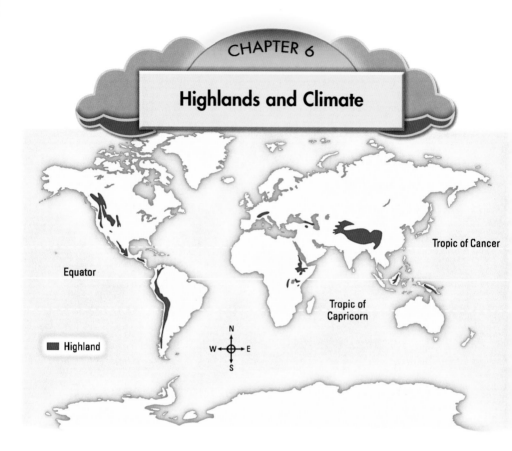

CHAPTER 6

Highlands and Climate

It may be hard to believe, but places only a few miles apart can have different climates. This happens when the two places have different **altitudes.** Altitude is height above sea level. A single mountain can contain all three climate zones!

Temperature changes with altitude. The higher the place, the cooler the air is. Highlands are usually cooler than the lowlands of the same latitude.

Some tropical highlands have all three climate zones in one small area. The bottom of a high mountain near the equator has a tropical climate. Higher up, the mountain has a temperate area. At the very top, the mountain has a polar climate!

Highlands are very important for the lowlands around them. They store needed water. The snow on the mountains melts in spring and summer. It runs down onto the land below. This water is used by lowland plants and animals. Without it, they couldn't live and grow.

Three major highland areas are the Rocky Mountains of North America, the Himalaya Mountains of Asia, and the Andes of South America.

The Rocky Mountains

It is almost impossible to predict the weather in the Rocky Mountains. In just a few minutes, it can change from sunny to stormy. The weather also changes with altitude. For every 1000 feet (300 meters) that people climb, temperatures drop about 3 degrees. Sometimes hikers start out in warm weather, then run into a snowstorm as they climb higher.

Pike's Peak in the Rocky Mountains is covered with snow year-round.

Just as the climate changes with altitude, so do the plants. On the sunny south slopes and the moist north slopes between 7000 and 9500 feet (2130–2900 meters), many kinds of trees and flowers grow. Higher up grow pines that the wind has bent and twisted. Other trees grow next to large rocks that shelter them. The trees grow only as high as the rocks that protect them.

In the highest parts of the Rockies, few plants brave the cutting winds and bitter cold. Moss-like plants grow close to the ground. These plants have long roots. The long roots keep the wind from pulling the plants out of the ground. Some plants have thick leaves to protect them from the wind and cold.

Animal life in the Rockies also changes with altitude. Buffalo graze at the base of the mountains. Halfway up, mountain lions prowl. At the top, a lucky hiker will spot a golden eagle.

Bighorn sheep in the Rocky Mountains

35

The Himalaya Mountains

The highest peaks of the Himalaya Mountains are in Tibet. Most of this area is 12,000 feet (3657 meters) above sea level. Some parts reach more than 16,000 feet (4876 meters) in altitude. Summer temperatures are warm during the day but very cold at night. The Asian monsoon winds bring rain. Winters in the Himalayas are harsh. The snowfall is light, but temperatures are very low. Strong winds make the cold even harder to bear. The snow line (the line above which the snow doesn't melt) starts at about 20,000 feet (6096 meters).

Thousands of types of plants and animals live in the Himalayas. The foothills are covered in deciduous

Mount Everest in the Himalayas stands 29,028 feet (8848 meters) tall. It is the highest spot on Earth.

A Tibetan in the Himalayas

forests. Temperate forests grow in the middle altitudes. Higher up are pine and fir forests. Just below the snow line, the forests end and tough, low-growing plants take over.

Weather in the Himalayas changes with the seasons. When the seasons change, many animals migrate. They move to an area with milder weather and more food.

The Andes Mountains

The Andean highlands of South America lie on the equator, so they are in the tropics. The weather in these places is not warm, though. Because the Andes Mountains are so high, the weather is quite cool.

The Andes are home to many plants and animals. One fascinating part of the Andes is a misty, green area called the cloud forest. The cloud forest grows between 3000 and 11,000 feet (914 and 3353 meters). Warm, moist air rises from the Amazon basin. It meets the cold, dry mountain air and forms clouds, rain, and fog. These clouds stay over the forest almost all the time. Because there is plenty of water, many plants grow in the cloud forest.

Some very interesting animals live in the Andes. Llamas and alpacas are related to the camel. Andean stags are a kind of deer. They live in areas far from people's homes. The best-known animal of the Andes is the giant condor. It is the largest flying bird in the world. From tip to tip, its wings can measure up to 12 feet (3.7 meters). That's as long as some cars!

Alpacas in the Andes Mountains

CHAPTER 7

The Earth's Changing Climates

Weather changes from hour to hour and from day to day. Climate can also change, but the change happens very slowly. Changes in climate are caused by changes in the ocean and the sun's energy.

The earth absorbs energy from the sun. Then it returns the same amount of energy to space. This balance keeps the overall amount of energy on the earth the same.

Rain helps to keep the amount of energy on the earth the same. After it falls, it changes into gas and rises back into the air. When it **evaporates,** it returns heat to the atmosphere. Wind and ocean currents help to spread heat over the earth's surface.

Most people choose to live in places with a mild climate. As climates change over time, people have to change, too. A thousand years ago, the northern latitudes were not as cold as they are today. Vikings from Iceland settled on the southern coast of Greenland. Back then, it was warm enough to live there. Over the centuries, the climate got colder. The Vikings left their home. They went to find a milder climate.

Mayan ruins in Mexico

Scientists believe that a change in climate may have caused the fall of the Mayan civilization. The Maya lived in Central America and Mexico. Their civilization suddenly ended around 1200 years ago. Scientists took samples of sediment from the bottom of a lake in Mexico. These samples showed that the climate was getting drier when the Mayan civilization fell. A dry climate can cause **drought.** During a drought there is not enough water to grow crops.

Scientists have found signs that most of today's deserts were once full of people. The ruins of several great cities sit in places that are now deserts.

Why Climates Change

Sometimes nature causes climates to change. When large volcanoes erupt, they spew ash into the air. The ash blocks sunlight, and the earth's surface cools.

When ocean currents change, they can change climates on land. Sometimes parts of the Pacific Ocean get warmer than usual. The warmer water changes weather patterns around the world. This change in weather is called El Niño. During El Niño, the warmer water makes ocean **currents** change direction.

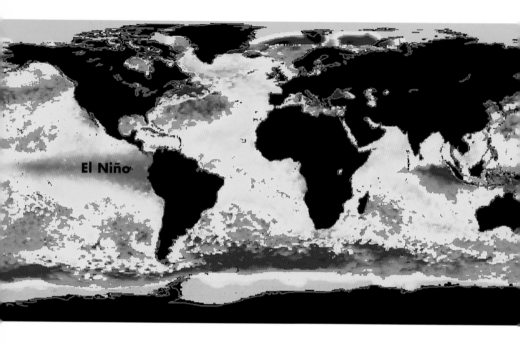

El Niño

El Niño can have serious effects. In 1982 and 1983, the surface temperature of the Pacific Ocean rose almost 7 degrees. Small fish called anchovies escaped to colder waters. Fishers who live in Peru couldn't find any fish to catch. Indonesia and Australia had a bad drought. Other parts of the world were affected differently. Typhoons occurred as far east as Tahiti. Ecuador and Peru were flooded with 300 times the normal amount of rain! In addition, the west coast of North America was much more stormy than it usually is.

How People May Be Changing Climates

Many scientists worry that people may be changing the earth's climates. We burn fossil fuels when we drive cars, heat buildings, and make electricity. When these fuels burn, they release carbon dioxide gas into the atmosphere. Carbon dioxide traps heat, so the earth can't send as much energy back up into the atmosphere. The energy stays near the earth's surface, raising temperatures. This process is called the greenhouse effect, or **global warming.** Global warming could change current patterns of rain and snow across the world.

Global warming could also melt the ice at the North and South poles. The melting ice would raise the sea level. The sea level has already risen 4–8 inches (10–20 centimeters) over the last 100 years. A higher sea level may change the ocean currents. In turn, the changes in the currents may cause more tropical storms. Even worse, scientists think that these tropical storms may be stronger than those of today.

The melting of polar ice would also have other effects. Many cities close to the ocean would be in danger. Places like New York and London could disappear beneath the sea!

Holes in the ozone layer around the earth add to global warming. The ozone layer is a layer of oxygen in the earth's atmosphere. It keeps harmful rays of sun from hitting the earth.

How We Can Protect Our Climates

People are working hard to understand climate change. They are taking steps to keep the climate from changing too much. Many cities and states are trying to cut down on the amount of harmful gases that they put into the air.

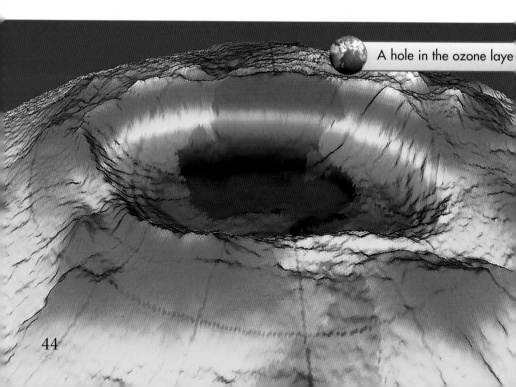

A hole in the ozone laye

**Ways to Reduce Carbon Dioxide
in the Atmosphere**

- Do not use aerosol products.
- Reduce, reuse, and recycle.
- Cut down on the use of electricity.
- Plant trees around your house. Trees help clean the air.

All of the climates of the world help to keep our planet healthy. So do the animals and plants that live in them. People can help, too. Some people don't think that one person can make a difference. But protecting the planet starts with one person at a time.

GLOSSARY

air pressure (AIR presh uhr) the weight of the atmosphere pressing on the earth

altitudes (AL tuh toodz) how high something is above the level of the sea

atmosphere (AT muhs fihr) the gasses around the earth

average (AV rij) usual or ordinary in amount or kind

blizzards (BLIZ uhrdz) heavy snowstorms

climate (KLY muht) the kind of weather an area usually has

condenses (kuhn DENS iz) changes to a liquid

cryosphere (KRY uh sfihr) the parts of the earth that are often covered by snow and ice

currents (KUHR uhnts) flows of moving water

cyclones (SY klohnz) very strong windstorms

deciduous (dih SIJ oo uhs) shedding its leaves in the fall

drought (drowt) a very long time without rain

equator (ih KWAY tuhr) a circle around the middle of the earth

evaporates (ih VAP uh rayts) changes into a gas

glaciers (GLAY shuhrz) rivers of ice

global warming (GLOH buhl WAWRM ing) a slow
rise in the earth's temperature

humidity (hyoo MID uh tee) the amount of water in
the air

latitude (LAT uh tood) distance north or south of
the equator

monsoons (mahn SOONZ) winds that blow over
large areas

precipitation (prih sip uh TAY shuhn) water that falls
from clouds to the earth's surface

scorches (SKAWRCH iz) burns the surface

taiga (TY guh) a type of climate where cone-bearing
trees are the main forms of life

tropics (TRAHP iks) the region of the earth that lies
on or near the equator

tundra (TUHN druh) a type of climate with frozen
soil and low-growing plants

water vapor (WAH tuhr VAYP uhr) water that has
been turned into a gas

INDEX